This Walker book belongs to:

_____

_____

_____

First published 1985 by Walker Books Ltd
87 Vauxhall Walk, London SE11 5HJ
This edition published 2011

2 4 6 8 10 9 7 5 3 1

This book has been typeset in New Baskerville Educational

Printed in China

British Library Cataloguing in Publication Data:
a catalogue record for this book is available from the British Library

ISBN 978-1-4063-3356-5

www.walker.co.uk

Bear's Birthday

Allan Ahlberg   Colin McNaughton

Bear's Birthday
Big Head
Open the Door

WALKER BOOKS
AND SUBSIDIARIES
LONDON • BOSTON • SYDNEY • AUCKLAND

Bear's Birthday

a bear

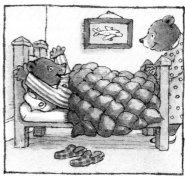

a happy bear

a happy birthday bear

a happy birthday bear
and his friends

a party

a happy party

a happy noisy party

a sad noisy bear

a happy bear

tickle
tickle

a happy ending

Big
Head

big head

little head

big ear

little ear

big eye   little eye

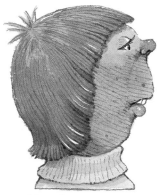

big nose   little nose

big mouth

little mouth

little hat

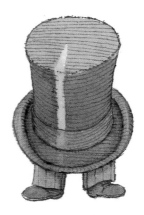

big hat

Open
the
Door

open the door

shut the door

open the window

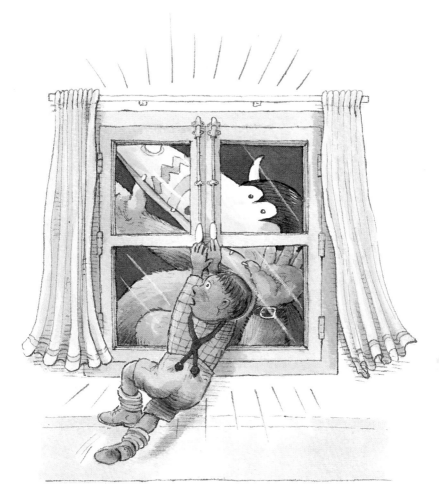

shut the window

open the fridge

shut the fridge

open the box

shut the box

open the parcel